Charlie Cook's Favourite Book

 For Alice, Alison and Alyx

First published 2005 by Macmillan Children's Books
This edition published 2006 by Macmillan Children's Books
a division of Macmillan Publishers Limited
20 New Wharf Road, London N1 9RR
Basingstoke and Oxford
Associated companies throughout the world
www.panmacmillan.com

ISBN: 978-1-4050-3470-8

25 27 29 30 28 26 24

A CIP catalogue record for this book is available from the British Library.

Printed in China

Charlie Cook's Favourite Book

Julia Donaldson

Illustrated by Axel Scheffler

MACMILLAN CHILDREN'S BOOKS

Once upon a time there was a boy
called Charlie Cook
Who curled up in a cosy chair
and read his favourite book . . .

About a leaky pirate ship
which very nearly sank
And a pirate chief who got the blame
and had to walk the plank.

The chief swam to an island
and went digging with his hook.

At last he found a treasure chest,
and in it was a book . . .

About a girl called Goldilocks,
and three indignant bears
Who cried, "Who's had our porridge?
Who's been sitting on our chairs?"

They went into the bedroom,
and Baby Bear said, "Look!
She's in my bed, and what is more,
she's got my favourite book . . ."

AS HE READ ALOUD A JOKE HE'D FOUND
(INSIDE HIS FAVOURITE BOOK)...

About Rowena Reddalot,
a very well-read frog,

Who jumped upon a lily pad

and jumped upon a log,

Then jumped into the library
which stood beside the brook,

30

 And went, "Reddit! Reddit! Reddit!"
as she jumped upon a book...

About an oak tree full of birds.
Each bird had built a nest
And they had a competition
to decide which one was best.

They chose an owl to judge it,
and the winner was a rook
Whose nest was lined with pages
from his very favourite book . . .

About a girl who saw

a flying saucer in the sky.

Some small green men were in it

and they waved as they flew by.

She tugged her mother's sleeve and said,

"Look, Mum, what I've just seen!"

But Mum said, "Hush, I'm trying to read

my favourite magazine . . ."

About a wicked jewel thief who stole the King's best crown

**But then got stuck
behind some sheep,
which slowed his
car right down.**

**The King dialled 999
and soon the cops
had caught the crook,**

SITUATIONS
VACANT

GOVERNESS required for
Lady Mary, aged 7. The child
is sadly quite contrary. She
insists she sees aliens in the
garden. A strict governess is
required, who can curb this
vivid imagination.

Apply with references to
Lady Fotherington, The Old
Rookery, Banbury Cross.

**And flung him into prison,
where he read his favourite book...**

About a greedy crocodile

who got fed up with fish

And went on land to try to find

some other kind of dish.

He went into a bookshop
and he there grew even greedier

While reading (on page 90
of a large encyclopedia) . . .

CAKE: a mixture of nice things, usually baked in the oven. It is eaten at teatime and on special occasions like birthdays and Christmas.

THE QUEEN'S BIRTHDAY CAKE

It took six lorries to carry the Cocoa Munchies for the Queen's birthday cake to the palace. The cake also required 4,276 bars of chocolate and 739 sackfuls of marshmallows. The special outsize cake tin was made by the Royal Blacksmith, using 2,647 melted-down horseshoes.

FAMOUS CAKE-EATERS

Britain's most famous cake-eaters are the Bunn twins of York. At the age of six they became the youngest ever winners of the York Festival Cake-Eating Competition. Aged ten, they had to be taken to hospital after knocking each other out, while both reaching for the same slice of cake. (Their dog then ate the cake.)

About the biggest birthday cake the world had ever seen. A team of royal cakemakers had made it for the Queen.

The cake was so delicious
    that a famous spaceman took
A slice of it to Jupiter.
    He also took a book . . .

About a ghost who glided round a castle every night,

Carrying her head and giving everyone a fright.

She kept it up till morning, then she found a shady nook

And put her head back on again
to read her favourite book...

About a cosy armchair,
and a boy called Charlie Cook.